The STONE HORSEMEN

Tales from the Caucasus

Pictures
by
Judith
Gwyn
Brown

The Stone Horsemen

Tales from the Caucasus retold by

RUTH FOSTER

The Bobbs-Merrill Company, Inc.
A Subsidiary of Howard W. Sams & Co., Inc.
Publishers · Indianapolis · Kansas City · New York

For Rick and Danny

CONTENTS

The Old
Storyteller

A LONG, LONG TIME AGO, a tired-looking old man rode slowly through the Caucasus Mountains on a magnificent horse. He wore a wide black cloak and a tall fur hat, and his beard was as white as the snow on the peaks above him. His piercing eyes and lined face made him look very wise.

His name had been forgotten long ago. He was known through all the valleys simply as the storyteller.

In this region of southern Russia more than fifty languages were spoken by tribes isolated from each other

1

and from the world—and he knew them all. He had spent his life going from village to village telling his stories.

He had crossed deep ravines and gorges cut by raging torrents. The wind howled down the passes as he made his way up the narrow, twisting paths of the bare peaks. He had passed through the dense, dark forests where no man had ever been.

Now he had grown quite old. It was becoming more and more difficult to ride through the savage country. The villages, called *auls*, perched high on the sides of the cliffs, were taking longer and longer to reach.

One day, on his way through the fierce mountains, he met a youth. Never had the old man seen anyone leap the ravines so fearlessly. The youth's cloak billowed out behind him as his horse raced down the steep path, and his dagger glistened in the sun.

"You are the young man I have been searching for," the old man said. "No one else could reach the villages in the valleys, separated by these fearsome ranges. No one else could climb to the *auls* sitting like eagles' nests near the peaks. Come with me and I shall teach you the history of these mountains and the stories its people tell."

The young man smiled doubtfully.

"I can leap gorges and ride a horse up the steep side of a mountain. I can find my way through the dark forests. My dagger is ready for any ferocious wolf," he said. "But I am no storyteller. Where would I find the words?"

"If you know the valleys and the lives of the moun-
taineers, the words will come," the old man said. "People have lived in these mountains since very ancient
times—long before this land between the Black and
Caspian seas became a part of Russia.

"The Caucasus has been besieged from all directions
through all of its history. Invaders and colonizers came
from Greece and Rome and all the empires of western
Asia. The thundering hordes of Genghis Khan and
Tamerlane swept down from the northeast.

"Terrified inhabitants seeking refuge from the invaders settled in the rugged mountains. Men from the attacking armies lost their way and settled in the gorges.
Each valley became the home of a new group, with its

own customs and its own language. On the plain these people would have merged, but here, in isolated gorges, each group remained distinct and suspicious. The men always went armed, and fortified their homes.

"People living in villages separated by only a ravine often spoke different languages. That village only two or three miles away was thought of as a foreign land. And that land, because it was unknown and hard to reach, was imagined to be filled with giant warriors and menacing dragons—and sometimes beautiful princesses."

"Are all your stories about adventures in strange lands?" asked the young man. "I heard a tale of how the mountains were formed from giants who fought a mighty battle before the time of man. And when the earth trembles beneath our feet, those rumblings are said to be the anger of the giants imprisoned now in stone."

"That is a legend," the old man said. "A story which tries to explain the world. Yes, I tell legends and animal stories, too. And most often of all funny stories that amuse and entertain—for everyone likes a clever fellow.

"Stop here with me, young man, and listen to some of the tales told by the many tribes living in these mountains. Then decide whether you will come with me and take my place when I can no longer climb the steep sides of the mountains."

The two men dismounted and prepared to camp for the night. Wrapped in their warm felt cloaks, they sat before the fire, and the old man began.

The Stone Horsemen

IN A SMALL VILLAGE, high in the mountains of Dagestan, lived three Avar sisters. One day a khan, riding back from the hunt, stopped at their cottage to rest. As he sat with his companions, joking and drinking wine, he overheard the girls whispering in the other room.

"If the khan were to marry me, I would weave cloth for the whole army from one bag of thread," said the oldest sister.

"If the khan married me, I would bake bread for the whole country from one measure of flour," said the middle one.

"If the khan were to marry me, I would bear him a son with teeth of pearls and a daughter with hair of pure gold," said the youngest sister.

Delighted by this conversation, the khan decided to marry the youngest girl. The bells rang out, the drums rolled, and the wedding was celebrated in great splendor. The young queen's eyes shone with happiness as she sat with her two sisters in the banquet hall.

The older girls, however, resented the good fortune of their sister deeply, and they waited for the day when they might do her harm.

Early in spring the khan left for the wars, because a powerful enemy was approaching his border. While he was gone, the queen bore him a son with teeth of pearls and a daughter with hair of pure gold.

One night, as the queen lay sleeping, the jealous sisters took the children from their cradle and had them thrown into a nettle-filled ravine. And the following day they sent a messenger to the khan with the news that the queen had given birth to a puppy and a kitten. The khan was furious and ordered the animals drowned and his wife chained to the city gates, so that all who entered would mock her.

Meanwhile, in the ravine, the cries of the babies were heard by a golden-horned doe. She fed them and cared for them till they were grown. Then she led them out of the ravine.

They walked for a long time until they reached a clearing in the midst of which stood an old castle.

"The time has come for us to part," said the doe. "Give me your word, young man, that you will speak to no one without keeping a handkerchief in front of your mouth; and you, young maiden, that you will show no one your golden hair. Otherwise, things will go badly with you."

They both promised, and the doe disappeared into the forest.

The youth, taking his sister by the hand, bravely entered the castle. They walked from one room to another, but they met not one living soul.

The boy busied himself hunting, while the girl remained behind, taking care of their new home.

One day, while she was bathing in a brook that ran near the castle, a golden hair fell from her head and the quick stream whirled it away.

This stream flowed through her father's capital, and an old woman, coming there for water, caught the golden hair. Admiring its brillance, she decided to take it to the khan.

News of this unusual find spread quickly. The jealous sisters realized that the boy and the girl had not perished in the ravine. They called the old woman to the palace, and the older of the sisters said, "The girl from whose head the golden hair has fallen has a brother. He is our sworn enemy. While he lives, we are in danger. Find out where they live, and see if you can get rid of him. We will reward you generously."

The woman agreed readily, and that very day set out in search of the girl with the hair of gold.

For many days she followed the stream and finally found herself in front of the castle. Near the doorway sat a young girl, and the wind played gently with her golden hair.

Catching sight of the old woman, the girl clapped her hands with joy at seeing another person, for she was very lonely. She forgot completely the warning of the doe.

"From where have you come, esteemed lady?" she asked.

"I have come from the land of a mighty khan," replied the old woman. "One day I caught a golden hair in a quick stream and took it to the palace. The khan has ordered me to find the girl from whose head the hair has fallen." The old woman looked about her. "Do you live here alone?" she asked.

"I live here with my brother, but he goes into the forest each day to hunt," replied the girl.

"I am sorry for you, pretty one, here all alone. A girl of your beauty should be living in luxury, surrounded by crowds of admirers. Come back with me."

"No," answered the girl. "I promised my brother never to leave the castle in his absence."

Then the clever old woman said, "In the east, in a marvelous valley, grows a magic apple tree. It talks to itself, and claps its branches, and while clapping, dances. Ask your brother to bring you a branch from this magic tree—it will keep you amused and happy."

After the golden-haired girl had thanked her, the old woman took her leave, promising to visit again.

When the brother returned from the forest, his sister said to him breathlessly, "They say that in the east, in a deep valley, there grows a magic apple tree. It talks to itself, claps its branches, and dances. Please bring me a branch from this marvelous tree; it will help me to pass the time alone."

The brother, unable to resist his sister's pleas, mounted his horse and rode off to find the magic tree.

After riding many days, he reached the deep valley. Its entrance was guarded by two gigantic cliffs. At intervals they collided violently, and the roar through the valley was deafening.

The youth spurred his horse and soared into the air. The thundering cliffs came together, but he had already passed through unharmed. He broke a branch from the magic tree, thrust it into his belt, and spurring his horse on, he again leaped high into the air. The cliffs roared together, but they succeeded only in cutting off the tip of his horse's tail. And the youth rode back to his sister.

The golden-haired girl played contentedly with the remarkable branch, and the youth went hunting as before.

Again the old woman came to visit. She found the girl sitting in front of the castle, playing with the magic branch.

"Good day, young lady, and how are you?" she asked.

"Oh, thanks to you, I am very happy and no longer bored. My brother brought me this marvelous plaything, and with it the days pass quickly."

"I am sorry for you, pretty one. Sooner or later this toy will lose its charm. All girls have friends, but you are always alone. I have heard that across the mountains, in a silver palace, lives a princess named Zulkhar. There is no more beautiful maid in this wide world. If your brother were to marry her, you would have a friend."

When the brother returned, the girl begged him to marry the Princess Zulkhar. She so praised her beauty that the youth decided to do as she asked.

He mounted his horse, bade his sister farewell, and rode off.

He passed through many lands, but nowhere did he meet anyone who had heard of the beautiful Princess Zulkhar. One morning, riding along the narrow path, he overtook an old man.

"Have you heard, O honored sir, of the beautiful Princess Zulkhar?" he asked.

"Yes, I have," replied the old man. "She lives on the other side of the mountains, in a silver palace surrounded on all sides by water. Do not go there, my son! Many brave youths have ridden that road, and not one of them has returned. Terrible peril awaits you there."

"Only cowards run from danger," bravely answered the youth, and he spurred his horse onward.

The old man looked after him, and shook his head sadly.

The youth crossed the high ridge of mountains and saw before him the silver palace of the beautiful Princess Zulkhar.

The shore of the river was full of horsemen, standing strangely still. Going closer, the young prince saw that the riders had all been turned to stone. Fear gripped him, and for a moment he thought of turning back. Then he steeled himself, stood tall in his stirrups, and shouted as loudly as he could.

"Princess Zulkhar!"

There was no answer. The young man felt a strange coldness touch his knees. His legs had turned to stone.

He shouted a second time. Again there was no answer. The young man turned to stone to his waist.

Summoning his last drop of strength, the youth shouted for the third time. The Princess Zulkhar did not answer, and the youth turned to stone from head to foot.

The river ran on serenely, and on the shore stood a new stone rider.

At home the sister waited for her brother. She waited and waited, but he did not return. A month passed, a second, and a third, and still he did not come. Her heart was seized with fear. Something terrible must have happened.

She put iron soles on her boots, and set out in search of the young prince with teeth of pearls.

She walked and walked. She walked for many days and nights, until she finally met the old man who had advised her brother not to ride to the silver palace of the beautiful Zulkhar.

"Where are you going, young maiden?" he asked.

"I am searching for my only brother. Three months ago he rode off to marry the beautiful Princess Zulkhar, and he has not come back."

"Many brave young men have set out on that road, but not one of them has returned. They have all been turned to stone on the shore of the enchanted river. Your brother must have suffered the same sad fate."

"Is there not some way to bring them back to life?" asked the girl.

"Yes, there is," answered the old man. "If you can make the beautiful Zulkhar answer your call and show her face, the magic spell will be broken, and the stone horsemen will come to life."

"I am ready to try," declared the golden-haired girl bravely, and she started off.

She walked and walked. Days and nights she walked. The iron soles of her boots wore out, but she did not stop until she reached the silver castle of the beautiful Zulkhar.

On the shore she saw her brother among the stone riders. She touched the cold body of the handsome youth and heavy tears fell from her eyes. She turned and faced the silver palace.

"O cruel Zulkhar! You have taken my only brother from me. Answer my call!"

But the princess did not appear, and the golden-haired girl felt her legs grow cold as she turned to stone to her knees.

She looked down with horror at her stone feet, and shouted,

"O Zulkhar! Is your *heart* made of this cold stone? I beg you to answer my call!"

But Zulkhar did not answer, and the golden-haired girl turned to stone to her waist.

A deadly fear entered her heart, and summoning her last drop of strength, she shouted,

"O proud Zulkhar! Are you *afraid* to come out? Are you *sure* you are more beautiful than I?"

The tightly closed doors of the silver castle swung open, and a drawbridge fell into place. The beautiful Zulkhar came across, shouting as she ran:

"Who dares compare herself to me?"

"I do," answered the girl. And she pulled the veil from her head. Her long hair spilled down her back like a river of gold.

At that moment the stone riders came to life. With a joyous shout, the youth rushed to his sister and embraced her.

The beautiful Zulkhar, dazzled by his smile, walked up to him, and asked,

"Tell me, young man, which of us is the more beautiful?"

The youth looked at the two girls standing before him and laughed.

"There is no need to compare you," he said. "The golden-haired girl is my sister, and you will be my wife."

All the revived horsemen were invited to the wed-

ding, and that very evening they joyfully celebrated
the marriage of the handsome prince with the teeth of
pearls to the beautiful Princess Zulkhar.

In the morning, the youth, his wife, and his golden-
haired sister rode off to their castle in the forest.

There the three lived peacefully together. When Zulkhar heard the story of their past, and of the promise
they had given the doe never to reveal the teeth of the
youth nor the hair of the maiden, she exclaimed,

"Why have you broken your word? You must swear
never again to risk danger by going about uncovered."
From that time the youth kept his mouth covered with
a handkerchief and the girl hid her hair beneath a veil.

The two girls remained at the castle, enjoying each
other's company, while the youth went hunting as before.

One day the young prince met a group of travelers
lost in the forest. Among them was the khan. The youth
invited the weary party to rest and refresh themselves
at the castle.

The khan, grateful for the hospitality shown him,
asked the three young people to be his guests at his
palace.

Early the next morning they all mounted their horses
and started out. When they reached the gates of the
city, they saw the queen chained to the wall.

"What terrible thing has this woman done, to be so
severely punished?" the young man asked.

The khan told them the story of the birth of his children. The beautiful Zulkhar, on hearing his words,

understood who her husband really was. She tore the handkerchief from the young man's mouth and the veil from his sister's head. The khan stared in amazement as his son smiled his wonderful smile and his daughter's golden hair shone in the sunlight.

The sister and brother threw themselves at their mother with a cry. The heavy chains clanked as the unfortunate woman held out her arms.

The khan fell down on his knees before his wife and begged her forgiveness.

"Come back to the palace," he pleaded. "I shall spend my life atoning for my cruelty."

The good heart of the queen relented at the sight of his distress, and she and her children and the beautiful Princess Zulkhar proceeded to the palace of the khan.

In the evening a great feast was held. Rivers of wine flowed, and the guests made merry far into the night.

The Stupid
Wolf

ONE EVENING A HUNGRY WOLF walked out of the forest
and met a donkey.

"Donkey," said the wolf, "I'm going to eat you!"

"Wolf, I am in your power. I am not strong enough
to resist you. But is it possible you don't know that a
donkey can be eaten only in the morning?" asked the
donkey in surprise. "The meat of a donkey is deadly
poison at night. Why don't you wait here? I will bring
a bed for you to sleep on. When you awaken it will be
morning, and you can eat me then."

"It's very kind of you to warn me," said the wolf. "Go and bring the bed. I'll wait here till you return."

The donkey ran off and the wolf settled down to wait. He waited and waited, but the donkey did not come back. "Where can that animal be?" wondered the wolf. It was not until he saw the sun creep into the sky that he realized he had been fooled.

The hungry wolf was very angry. "I will eat the very next thing I see!" he growled.

As he loped along, he met a little goat coming down the road. "Hey there, goat! I am going to eat you!" he shouted.

"I am completely in your power," humbly answered the goat. "But what kind of taste will my meat have without garlic? Allow me to run home and get some for you."

"You're right," agreed the wolf. "I have heard that goat meat is delicious with garlic. It was good of you to remind me. Go ahead, but see that you return quickly!"

The little goat ran off and the wolf settled down to wait. He waited and waited, but the goat did not return. How that wolf gnashed his teeth when he realized he had been fooled again!

Running more slowly, for he was very hungry, he came to the shore of the sea. There he saw an old buffalo wallowing in a pool of mud.

"Buffalo," shouted the wolf, getting ready to spring, "say good-by to life! I have come to eat you!"

The buffalo raised his head slowly. "Why are you

jumping about and shouting so?" he asked lazily. "You know I can't escape. I thought you were a clever animal. It would be smarter for you to say, 'Go on, buffalo, take a swim. I can't eat anything as muddy as you.' "

"You're certainly very muddy," agreed the wolf. "Go and bathe. But don't stay in the water too long—I haven't eaten for two days and I'm very hungry."

"Don't worry," said the buffalo, and he waded into the sea.

The wolf sat down on the shore and watched as the buffalo swam farther and farther out.

"Buffalo," shouted the wolf, "you're clean enough! Have you forgotten that I'm waiting?"

The buffalo laughed. "I haven't forgotten," he said. And he swam away.

The wolf was furious at having lost another dinner. He started back for his home in the forest, hungrier than ever.

Tired and discouraged, his pride wounded and his paws sore, he lay down to rest on the grass. Suddenly he saw a horse. "This one won't get away from me!" exclaimed the wolf.

With his last drop of strength, he sprang at the horse. "Horse," he said, "I am going to eat you!"

"You're very strong," said the horse. "I know I cannot escape. But I have one request to make before you eat me. Have pity and allow me to keep a promise I made to my father."

"What kind of promise?" asked the wolf impatiently. "I am very hungry and I have no time for words."

"My father warned me that I must not die without knowing how old I am. The day and year of my birth are stamped on my rear shoes. Take a look, dear wolf, and tell me my age. Then you may do what you wish with me."

"Very well," agreed the wolf. "I suppose I can do that for you." He stood in back of the horse. "Show me your shoes," he said.

The horse raised his hind legs. He kicked that foolish wolf on his foolish head and the blow sent him sailing through the air. I don't know where he landed, but he was never seen in Dagestan again.

The Brave
Shepherd Boy

THE SEEMINGLY ENDLESS HORDES of the terrible Timur
swept down upon a sandy plain in Dagestan. They had
come thousands of miles across the steppes of Central
Asia, overpowering all in their path. Now, tired and
thirsty, they stared at the empty sands and bare cliffs.

They set up their tents and Timur sent caravans in
all directions to look for water. The thirsty men lay
expectantly, unable to sleep, as they waited for the return of the camels.

Slowly, one after another, the caravans came back.

But they brought no water. They had found not one river, not one lake, not even a tiny spring.

Timur shook with rage.

"Let the leaders of the caravans come forward!" he shouted.

The men stood before him, filled with fear at the sight of his anger.

"The roads we traveled were all empty," they said. "All the inhabitants have fled to the hills and the villages were deserted."

Timidly, a tall old man stepped forward. In a quavering voice he said, "I met a shepherd boy along the way. Knowing he must get water for his sheep somewhere nearby, I questioned him. But he would tell me nothing."

"What have you done with him? Did you let him go?" demanded Timur.

"No, great sir! We tied him up and brought him back with us."

"Bring that shepherd boy to me!" thundered Timur.

"Do you know who I am?" he growled when the lad stood before him.

"Yes, you are Tamerlane the Earth-Shaker, conqueror of the world," answered the boy.

"Do you know I can do anything I wish with you?"

"Yes, I know."

"Then show my men where you get the water for your sheep, so that my warriors may quench their thirst!"

The boy did not answer.

"I order you to tell me!" shouted Timur.

The boy took his cloak from his shoulders.

"I have already been ordered by your men," he said, displaying the marks of the whip on his back.

"I tried to beat it out of him, but he stood as one made of stone," said the leader of the caravan.

Timur advanced threateningly on the boy. "We shall see what kind of stone he is made of!"

At his words a strange chill was felt by Timur and his warriors. They stared in horror as the boy turned to stone before their eyes. They could never hurt him now.

They were badly frightened, and despite their thirst and fatigue, the tents were struck and the army of Timur departed as quickly as it could.

The stone boy was left standing on the dry sands, his cloak thrown over his shoulders, his tall sheepskin hat upon his head. And there he stands to this day.

A Strange
Choice

THERE LIVED A MAN in a Chechen *aul* who had a most beautiful wife. They were so poor that often they did not have enough to eat. In spite of this, the wife loved her husband, Achmed, dearly, and they lived very happily together.

The chief of the village was very much taken by the beauty of Achmed's wife. He tried in every way to persuade her to leave her husband, but this the young woman would not do.

One especially hard day in the life of Achmed he

went into the forest to collect firewood. Coming to a clearing, he saw two ripe watermelons lying on the ground. Overjoyed, Achmed took one of them and returned home to share his lucky find with his wife.

"A watermelon is a rare thing in our locality. Wouldn't it be better to sell it and buy bread with the money? Go to the chief and offer the melon to him," she said. "He surely will buy it."

"That's a fine idea," agreed Achmed. And he proceeded to the chief's house.

The chief paid him generously for the watermelon.

"Do you have another such melon?" he asked.

And Achmed answered, "Yes, there is one more."

"Bring it to me. In return, you may take whatever you first put your hand on in my house," said the chief. "But if you do not bring me the melon, I shall take the first thing I touch in your house."

Achmed ran home. "Wife," he cried joyfully, "the chief and I have agreed that if I bring him the other melon, I can take the first thing I touch in his house. I have decided to touch the trunk in which he keeps his gold. That will mean the end of our poverty!"

"Run quickly to the clearing," said the wife, "before someone else makes off with the melon. You realize that if you do not bring it to him the chief will touch *me* and take me for his wife."

The crafty chief had indeed sent two of his servants to follow Achmed, and they overheard all that was said by the couple.

The servants ran quickly to the clearing. By the

time Achmed arrived there, the melon was gone.

"What shall I do now?" thought Achmed with horror. "Now I must give my dear wife to the chief. No, I could never do that!"

Beside himself with grief, Achmed decided to run away. Filled with despair, he walked and walked until he finally reached a large city. As he stopped to rest near the gates, a man mounted on a magnificent horse rode by, and, seeing Achmed, stopped.

"Why do you sit here?" inquired the rider. But Achmed could only shake his head. He was too filled with despair to answer.

Touched by such sadness, Kenaf Ali, for this was the man's name, invited Achmed to be his guest. He enjoyed entertaining strangers, and he took Achmed home with him, where they became good friends.

One day the khan who ruled this city sent a messenger to Kenaf with an invitation to a banquet.

"Tell the khan I cannot attend because I have a distinguished visitor staying with me," said Kenaf.

The messenger left, and Kenaf said to Achmed, "I know that the khan will invite you to the banquet, too. Accept the invitation and we shall go together. But you must do exactly as I tell you or things will not go well.

"When we arrive, and the khan has greeted you, sit down next to him and do not give up your place to anyone who comes in after you."

Kenaf handed Achmed a carved ivory-hilted knife in a gold-mounted silver scabbard. "Take this knife," he said, "but do not allow anyone else to handle it.

During the feast use it to cut the meat, but when the others wash their knives, you must clean yours out of sight. If you do not do this, things will go badly for you."

Soon the khan's messenger returned, asking Kenaf to bring his guest to the banquet with him.

The khan greeted them warmly when they arrived, seating Achmed next to him, in the place of honor. Achmed bowed importantly and sat down.

The guests continued to arrive, and the khan greeted each of them. To some he gave his hand, to others he merely nodded. Achmed forgot the admonition of his friend and gave his place to each new guest in turn. Thus, at the beginning of the feast, he found himself at the other end of the hall.

The servants brought in the roasted ram and each guest cut a piece for himself with his own knife. One of the diners, having forgotten his knife, asked a servant standing behind him to bring him one.

Achmed, forgetting his friend's warning, offered the one he was using. The guest accepted gratefully. Looking at the knife, he marveled at its beauty and it was passed from hand to hand to be admired by all the guests.

Finally, it reached the khan. He looked at the ivory hilt and shrieked with fury. "Whose knife is this?"

The guests pointed to Achmed.

"I have finally found the thief! This knife was stolen from me, and I have sought the guilty one everywhere. Now he is finally in my hands! Seize him!"

The servants threw themselves on the hapless Achmed and tied his hands behind his back.

"O great khan! Put this worthless one into my hands —after all, I am responsible for bringing him here," begged Kenaf.

"Very well, I place him in your custody. But give me your word to guard him carefully, and give him no advice that will enable him to escape my vengeance," said the khan.

"I swear to you by the beard of Allah I shall not say one word to him!" promised Kenaf. And taking Achmed, he led him home.

All night the friends sat silent, unable to sleep. Achmed could think of nothing but his terrible misfortune, and Kenaf tried to think of how he might save

Achmed without breaking his word to the khan.

Suddenly Kenaf's cat jumped onto his lap.

"Pussycat, pussycat! You weak animal," said Kenaf. "With one blow of my hand I could kill you, and you, foolish cat, could not escape. If you were clever you would get up before dawn tomorrow, put on my finest coat, take my best weapons, seat yourself on my best horse, and ride to the khan.

"You know, at heart, the khan is as timid as a rabbit. Seeing your drawn brows and fierce frown, he would ask, 'What are you doing here?' And you would say to him, 'I, Khan, am searching for the murderer of my brother. From his dead body I took the knife you claim as your own. I have come to avenge my brother's death!'

"The khan would tremble at your words, and he would offer you a settlement. And you would take this money and return to me. Now scat, stupid animal, but watch out! If you do anything wrong, you will die!"

Achmed listened to the man murmuring to his cat, not daring to utter a sound. In the morning he did everything Kenaf had advised the cat to do, and rode off to the palace of the khan.

Just as Kenaf had predicted, Achmed returned with a large purse filled with gold. After dividing the treasure, Achmed said, "You have been a wise and true friend. Perhaps you can tell me how I might save my wife from the clutches of the chief I told you about."

"That should not be difficult," answered Kenaf. "When you return home, build a two-story house. On the first floor put all your wealth, and on the second your wife. Build the staircase leading to the second story in such a way that it topples as soon as the chief puts his foot on the first step. In falling he will grab the railing with his hands, and you will be free of your promise."

Achmed, now grown rich beyond his wildest expectations, thanked his friend and gaily rode home. His wife met him in tears. The chief had been giving her no peace. Each time he had come, she had put him off. But he would not wait much longer.

Achmed set about building the two-story house. When it was finished, he sent word to the chief to come and take what he liked.

The old man, dressed in his finest clothing, placed

his hands in his pockets so as not to touch anything ac-
cidentally, and rushed to the house of Achmed.

Searching the lower floor and not finding the young
woman he had tried for so long to possess, he prepared
to climb to the second floor.

No sooner had he placed his foot on the first step than
the staircase gave way and the chief grabbed frantically
for the railing with his hands.

"A railing is a strange choice." Achmed laughed.
"But you are welcome to take it. My wife, however,
stays here with me."

An Ossete Riddle

A MAN AND A WOMAN chanced to meet one day on a winding mountain road. In one hand the man held a hen and in the other a walking stick. A copper caldron was strapped to his back, and a goat followed behind, attached to a rope around his waist.

They climbed the steep path until they came to a ravine. They could hear the rush of water far below and see the sharp rocks jutting from the sides. The only bridge was a log stretched across the abyss. The man prepared to cross.

34

"Oh, wait!" cried the poor woman. "I could not possibly balance myself on that narrow log. Please help me across. My daughter is expecting me, and I shall never be able to reach her without your help."

"How can I possibly help you?" replied the man. "On my back is a heavy caldron. In one hand I have a hen and in the other a stick, and on top of everything I am leading a goat. You will have to stay here if you are afraid."

The woman was in despair. How could she cross so wide a chasm without help? Yet clearly the man, encumbered as he was, could not add her to his burdens. What was she to do?

As she stood thinking, the man again prepared to cross. Suddenly she shouted, "Wait! I have an idea. Why not take your animals over first and then come back for me?"

"Foolish woman! The goat will wander too close to the edge and fall into the ravine. The hen will flap her wings and disappear into the thicket, and I shall be left with nothing."

The woman nodded. What he said was true. What was she to do?

Again the man gathered his possessions together and prepared to cross.

"Wait!" cried the woman. "I'll tell you what to do!"

He stopped and listened as she explained her plan. Then he laughed.

"You are indeed a clever one," he said. "I should never have thought of such a solution myself."

He quickly ran across the narrow log, stuck his staff into the ground, and tied the goat securely to it. Then he turned the caldron upside down and set the hen beneath it. Sure now that they were safe, he ran nimbly to the other side to help the woman across.

Unlucky
Mussah

MANY YEARS AGO, high in a Kabard mountain village, lived a young man named Mussah. He was strong and brave and did everything well. He could run without tiring, shoot without missing, but he had no luck. And without luck, no matter how far you run, you reach nothing worthwhile; no matter how straight you shoot, your bullets hit only crows.

Mussah became angry at his fate and said, "My good luck, where have you hidden? Lazy ones live happily, but I have been working hard all my life, and still good fortune eludes me." And he decided to go out into the wide world to seek a better fate.

Early the next morning, without saying good-by to anyone, Mussah left his native village.

He walked and walked until he finally reached the shore of the blue sea. On the sand he saw a large fish thrashing about, trying desperately to get back into the water. To his amazement, Mussah heard the fish plead in a human voice:

"Good youth, throw me into the sea. Until the end of my days I shall not forget I am your servant. Take one of my scales. When you are in trouble, burn it and I shall be with you in a minute, although you be on the top of Mount Elbrus, where the foot of man has not yet climbed."

Mussah felt sorry for the suffering fish, and, taking a scale, he returned him to the water and proceeded on his journey.

The road led him to the edge of a dark forest. As he started to make his way through the undergrowth, he heard the wild cry of an animal in pain. Following the sound, Mussah came upon a deer, one leg caught beneath a fallen tree, struggling vainly to free himself.

When the deer saw Mussah, he pleaded, "Free me, dear youth. Till the end of my days I shall not forget your goodness, and when you are in difficulty I shall help you. Take a hair from my hide. When you need me, burn it, and in an instant I shall be at your side."

Mussah pitied the animal, and, taking a hair from his

thick hide, he freed his imprisoned leg. The deer galloped off and Mussah continued on his way.

He walked and walked until he finally came to a tree
so tall its branches seemed to touch the sky. In the tree
was a nest in which some young birds were peeping
piteously. Mussah looked about and saw a huge snake
coiled near the trunk. He pulled out his dagger, and
with a single sweep cut off the head of the horrible
serpent.

Suddenly the sky darkened, the wind howled, and a
huge eagle lit on the top of the tree. She saw Mussah
and, unsheathing her iron claws, prepared to attack.

Then the nestlings spoke up, saying, "Do not hurt
him, Mother; he saved us from certain death. See, at
his feet, the body of the terrible serpent. The monster
would have slain us had it not been for this brave
youth!"

The eagle hid her sharp claws, and taking a feather
from her wing, said, "As a reward for your goodness,
take this feather. If you are ever in trouble, burn it, and
no matter where you are, I shall come to your aid."

Mussah thanked the bird for her gift and continued
his journey.

He walked and walked until he finally came to the
wide, endless steppe. There he saw a pack of hunting
dogs, followed by their masters, racing in pursuit of a
black fox.

The fox ran straight toward Mussah, who grabbed
him and said, "Well, now I shall have a warm winter
hat!"

"Do you really need a hat so badly? Let me go, good youth," said the fox. "In my black coat there is one white hair. Find it and pull it out. When you are in trouble, burn this hair, and I shall immediately come to your aid."

Mussah pitied the black fox, and taking the white hair from the black fur, he let him go.

He walked and walked. He walked for many days and nights until he finally came to a large city.

In the center of the city stood a gleaming palace surrounded by an iron fence, and on each spike was a human head.

Mussah walked up to an old woman standing nearby.

"Dear Grandmother, why are these heads decorating the khan's fence?" he asked.

"You must be from a very far country if you do not know of this custom," she answered. "The khan has an only daughter. In all our land there is no maiden to equal her in beauty. But this princess is so proud, she can find no husband she thinks worthy of her. To everyone who comes to win her, she promises her heart if he can hide himself three times without her finding him. If she discovers him, there is no hope for the youth; the cruel khan orders his head cut off and placed on an iron spike. Ninety-nine heads have fallen and there are no more brave ones left to try their luck."

"Perhaps I should try," said Mussah thoughtfully.

"Go ahead, if you have a head to spare!" And the old woman walked away in great disgust.

Mussah decided this might be the very place to find

his good fortune. He straightened his hat and entered the palace.

"Good day," he said to the princess. "I have come to try my luck at winning your hand."

"Very well, go ahead. You have three chances to hide from me. If I cannot find you, I shall take you for my husband; but if you cannot hide successfully, your head will make one hundred that decorate my father's fence."

Mussah left the palace, walked to the edge of the sea, and burned the scale of the fish.

The sea roared and the fish swam up to the shore. "How can I serve you, good youth?" asked the fish.

"I am in terrible trouble," replied Mussah. "You must hide me so that no one in all the world will be able to find me."

"Well, that is a simple request. Jump into my mouth. I shall swim to the bottom of the sea and not a living soul will find you."

Mussah entered the mouth of the tremendous fish and the fish swam to the bottom of the wide, wide sea.

And the princess lifted her magic spyglass and began her search for Mussah. She probed every corner of the earth. She examined the sky. She did not see him anywhere.

"The clever one must have hidden in the bottom of the sea," said the princess with annoyance, and she aimed her spyglass at the depths of the sea.

And there sat Mussah, in the mouth of the fish, afraid to breathe.

At this moment a school of tiny fish swam by. Unable to resist such dainty morsels, the fish forgot himself, opened his huge mouth, and the princess saw Mussah.

"Come out! Come out!" she screeched. "I have found you!"

Sadly Mussah emerged and returned to the palace.

"Well, hide yourself a second time," ordered the princess.

Mussah went into the dark forest, burned the hair from the deer's hide, and in a moment that animal stood before him.

"How can I serve you, good youth?" asked the deer.

"I am in terrible trouble," answered Mussah. "Hide me so that no one in all the world can find me."

"Jump on my back. My cave is on the top of Mount Kazbek. There, not a living soul will be able to find you."

Mussah jumped on his tall back and the deer galloped swiftly to the top of the mountain peak. Mussah entered the cave, and the deer lay down at the entrance, shielding the opening of the cave with his body.

The princess searched the earth. She searched the heavens. She searched the depths of the sea. But she could not find Mussah.

"I think I shall look for him in the dark caves of the mountains," said the princess. And she lifted her magic spyglass to the hills.

And Mussah lay in the cave and was afraid to move.

At this moment a fly lit on the nose of the deer. Unable to control himself, he tossed his head. Then the princess saw Mussah and shouted, "Come out! Come out! I have found you!"

Mussah emerged from the cave and returned to the palace in great distress. Two chances were gone.

"Well, hide yourself for the last time!" taunted the princess.

Sadly Mussah walked to the wide meadow and burned the eagle feather. At that moment, the huge bird swooped down from the sky.

"How can I serve you, good youth?" she asked.

"A black day has indeed come upon me. Hide me so that no living soul can find me."

"That is a simple thing to do. Sit on my back and hold on tightly. I shall hide you where no one in all the world will discover you."

Mussah sat on the eagle's back, grasped her tightly around the neck, and the bird flew high above the clouds.

"Now no one can see you," she said.

Mussah stretched out and fell fast asleep, and the bird circled lazily above the clouds.

The princess searched the earth. She searched the sky. She searched the depths of the sea and all the mountain caves. She could find Mussah nowhere.

"Where could he have hidden?" thought the princess with annoyance. "Could he have flown above the clouds?"

She lifted her spyglass, and at that moment a furious

wind began to blow. It tore apart the clouds, and the princess saw Mussah, sleeping peacefully on the back of the eagle.

"Wake up! Wake up! You have slept away your life!" shouted the princess, and she ordered Mussah to come down.

"Well, Mussah, you, too, have lost," she said, as she prepared to summon the executioner.

"O beautiful princess! If it is fated that my head fall, it will fall, but I think my fate is to marry you. Let me hide just one more time!"

The princess, looking at the brave and handsome Mussah, could not refuse him, and she agreed to one last chance.

Mussah went out and burned the white hair. In an instant the black fox stood before him.

"How can I serve you, good youth?" he asked.

"If you cannot save me from the clever princess, my head will decorate the khan's fence. Hide me so that she cannot find me anywhere."

"That will not be hard to do," said the fox. "Wait here."

And the black fox turned and began to dig. His small paws scratched the earth so fast, a cloud of dust flew up behind him and he disappeared from view. Mussah grew uneasy as he waited, but the fox was back very soon.

"Follow me," he said. Mussah bent and entered the dark tunnel. He made his way as quickly as he could through the cramped passage which led straight to the palace. There the fox had hollowed out a cave beneath the very room in which the princess sat.

"Stay here and do not move," whispered the fox. "When you finally hear the khan's daughter admit she cannot find you anywhere, reach up and push aside the carpet. When you climb out, you will be in her room."

Meanwhile the princess walked to the window and raised her spyglass. She searched for Mussah over the earth. She searched the blue sea and the mountain caves. She searched far above the clouds. She could find him nowhere. And all the time Mussah was so close he could hear the rustle of her dress as she paced the room impatiently. He could hear her mutter as she tried to think of where he might be hiding.

Finally, the annoyed princess threw her magic spyglass to the ground. "This time he has outsmarted me!" she cried. "I cannot think of one other place to look."

When Mussah heard this, he raised the edge of the carpet and boldly entered the room.

Then the cannon boomed and the drums rolled, and the *lucky* Mussah married the proud princess.

Who Is Strongest?

ONE DAY THE BRAVE HUNTER MURZEL rode into the mountains of Svanetia and killed a goat. As he stood admiring his prize, the sky grew dark. He heard thunder, and great bolts of lightning flashed across the sky. A tall, century-old oak splintered into a thousand tiny slivers.

Lifting his face to the sky, Murzel shouted, "O you mighty white lightning! There is nothing in the world more powerful than you. I offer you my goat as a sacrifice."

Then the lightning answered, "No, Murzel, I am not the strongest of all. Look at the white head of Mount Elbrus. For many thousand years I have shot my fiery bolts at him, and still he stands as if untouched."

Then Murzel went to stand before Elbrus. "O white-crested Elbrus! You are the mightiest lord in all the world! Take from me this gift of my goat."

"No, Murzel. Water is far stronger than I am. Look at the gorges it has cut into my sides. My deep ravines and wide abysses have all been caused by the waters."

Then Murzel went to the mighty mountain torrent.

"O great mountain stream! You are the strongest in all the world. Take from me this gift of my goat."

"No, Murzel," answered the stream. "I am a son of the clouds; it is they who control the waters of the earth."

Murzel then climbed to the top of the mountain and said: "O mighty clouds! From you came the all-destroying waters. Take from me this goat as a sacrifice to your great power."

"No, Murzel," answered the clouds. "My ruler is the wind. He carries me wherever he wishes, and I must obey him without question."

Then Murzel went down into the valley and asked the wind, "Wind, are you not the strongest in all the world? You fell tall trees; the menacing clouds obey you. Take from me this goat as an offering to your power."

"No, Murzel," answered the wind. "I am not the strongest in the world. No matter how hard I try, I cannot tear nor crush the small green grass. It is stronger than I am."

Murzel bowed to the grass. "O green grass! It is said that you are stronger than the wind. If this be so, take from me this goat in your honor."

"Oh, Murzel, if I were truly strong, would I allow the sheep to eat me and crush me with their hoofs?"

Then Murzel went to the sheep and said, "Is it really true, sheep, that you are the strongest in the world and I must bring you my goat as a sacrifice?"

"No, Murzel," answered the sheep. "The butcher is stronger. He can slaughter us whenever he wishes."

Angrily Murzel went to the butcher and asked: "Butcher, are you really the strongest in the world? Must I sacrifice my goat to you?"

"What is the matter with you, Murzel? Even the mice are stronger than I am. They have completely destroyed my shop, and I don't know what to do about them!"

Amazed, Murzel went to the mice. "Mice, mice, are you really the strongest in the world? Must I offer you my goat?"

"What is the matter with you, Murzel? You know the cat is stronger than we are. We hide from her in every crack."

Murzel shook his head and went to find the cat.

"Cat, cat, they say you are the strongest in all the world and I must offer you my goat."

"Yes, that is true. I, the cat, am the strongest in the world. I am afraid of no one. My spine is as taut as a bow. My eyes glow like hot coals. My claws are like

sharp knives and my teeth are as strong as iron. Give me your goat!"

Murzel could stand no more. Angrily he grabbed the cat by the scruff of the neck and hurled her into the abyss.

As for the goat—he ate that himself.

Djamukh—
Son of a Deer

ONE BRIGHT SUNNY DAY, the hunter Shanba went into the dark Abkhaz forest in search of game. As he came to a clearing in the woods, he saw a deer. Raising his arm, he prepared to shoot, when a sudden movement near the deer caught his eye.

Shanba crept closer and saw a child sitting on the ground. He shouted, and the deer leaped into the thicket, leaving the little boy behind.

At the hunter's approach the child looked up curiously. Shanba knelt beside him. "Who are you? How came you into the forest?" he asked. The little boy babbled and laughed but he said not a word, and Shanba realized that he knew no human language.

Having no children, Shanba decided to take him home and bring him up as his own. He called him Djamukh—which means son of a deer.

The boy was bright and gay and grew quickly. When he learned to speak he explained that the deer had found him in the forest and had raised him with her fawn. He could not remember how he had gotten there nor who his family was. Djamukh grew to be a handsome and intelligent young man, wise in the ways of the forest and of men, and Shanba was very proud of his adopted son.

The years passed, and one day Shanba called Djamukh to him and said, "Dear son, death is knocking at the door of our home and the time for parting has come. Here is the key to the house. Everything within it now belongs to you. Everything, except the small chest which stands beneath my bed. If you do not wish to tempt fate, throw it in the river, I beseech you." With these words Shanba died, and Djamukh was left alone and lonely.

One day, roaming sadly through the empty house, he found himself with the chest in his hands. "What harm could befall me if I open it?" thought Djamukh, and he lifted the lid. Lying within was the portrait of a wide-eyed maiden.

From that time on Djamukh lost all peace of mind. The image of the beautiful girl was before him day and night. "Though she live in the depths of the sea, I must find this maiden," said Djamukh. And that very day he set off on his search.

Walking along the slope of the high mountain, he met a shepherd guarding a flock of rabbits. In his hand was a thin staff and on his feet were huge, heavy millstones. At Djamukh's approach the rabbits scampered off in all directions. The shepherd sprang after them, leaping from cliff to cliff with the fleetness of a deer, and in an instant he had gathered his flock together again.

Djamukh looked on with amazement. "How can you run so fast with millstones on your feet?" he asked.

"If I were to take them off, I would then gallop faster than the wind," answered the shepherd.

"I am searching for a girl who has enslaved my heart," said Djamukh, showing him the picture. "Would you like to come with me?"

"Yes, indeed," said the shepherd. "Perhaps I can be of service to you."

Djamukh agreed happily, and the two young men set off on their journey.

Along the road Djamukh inquired of each passer-by if any of them could tell him where the beautiful maiden might be found. But no one could help him.

Then in the deep forest they met a man lying on the ground, his ear pressed to the earth.

"Whatever are you doing?" asked Djamukh.

"Far away at the edge of the forest two ants are quarreling; I wish to know how they settle their differences," answered the stranger.

The amazed Djamuhk thought, "If only I had such a companion!"

And the stranger, as if he were reading his thoughts, asked, "Where are you off to, young man?"

"I am going in search of a beautiful maiden," answered Djamukh, and he showed him the picture of the beautiful girl.

"Take me with you. Perhaps I can be of service to you," offered the stranger.

Djamukh agreed, and the three marched merrily ahead.

Soon they came upon a man climbing a tree. He took an egg out from under a bird sitting in her nest. He did this so deftly, the bird never stirred.

"Where are you all going?" he asked as he descended with the egg.

"We are on our way to find a maiden for our friend Djamukh. Wouldn't you like to come along with us?"

"With such stalwart young men I am ready to go anywhere," answered the stranger, and all four marched ahead.

On the way they met a gray-haired old man.

"Would you know, Grandfather, in which country this young maiden is to be found?" asked Djamukh, bringing out the picture.

"Beyond those mountains," answered the old man, pointing to the dimly visible range in the distance. "But I must warn you, terrible dangers await you there. This maiden has three brothers—giant warriors who guard her night and day."

Undaunted, Djamukh thanked the old man, and the four friends continued on their way. After many days they crossed the ridge and entered a luxuriant valley. There, in a field of flowers, stood an old castle. At the entrance sat the maiden whose portrait had captured Djamukh's heart. She was beautiful beyond belief. In back of her stood her three giant brothers.

Seeing the newcomers, one of them asked, "Who are you and what do you want here?"

"I am Djamukh, son of a deer, and these are my friends. I have come to ask for the hand of your sister in marriage."

The brothers exchanged glances, and the oldest then said,

"Djamukh, I promise you the hand of my sister if you perform three tasks we set for you. But if you fail, your head will fall from your shoulders."

"I am ready," agreed Djamukh.

"In the courtyard lies a stone. Split it in half!"

Djamukh stared, aghast. A boulder the size of a buffalo lay nearby. How could he possibly split it?

"If he were to wind a hair from my head around his sword, the stone would split as easily as an apple," whispered the girl to herself.

The sharp-eared friend of Djamukh overheard her words and repeated them to the nimble-fingered one. He crept up beside the girl and gently lifted a fallen hair from her shoulder.

Djamukh wrapped the thin hair around his sword and struck the stone. The boulder split into two even

parts. From its center flew a black bird with a golden crest. He soared into the sky, smoothly described three circles above the head of Djamukh, and was lost from sight.

Then the second giant said, "Three days' journey from our castle there is an island. On its shore grow strange and beautiful flowers. I shall send my fastest runner for some, and you must do the same. If your runner should return before mine—take my sister for your wife."

"Very well," agreed Djamukh, and turning to the shepherd he said, "Save me, friend. Overtake the giant's runner."

"Don't worry, Djamukh. I won't be long," answered

the shepherd. He removed the millstones from his feet and was out of sight before the dust had settled.

The shepherd reached the island in just a few hours. He gathered the rare flowers and started back. On the way he met the giant's runner coming toward him. Seeing the shepherd, the runner shouted, "Hey there, friend! Wait a minute!"

The shepherd hid the flowers in his bag and stopped.

"I have met many runners in my time, but such speed as yours I have never seen. There is no faster racer than I in all this land and yet you are already on your way back. Let us drink to your quick heels," he said.

Before handing the wine to the shepherd, he surreptitiously slipped a powder into the cup. The shepherd, flattered by the praise of the racer, drank deeply. At that moment a deep sleep took possession of his body and he fell beside the road. The giant's runner tried to open the shepherd's bag but it was held so firmly, he could not pull it free. Annoyed, the runner sped off to the island to gather the flowers for himself.

Djamukh waited for the shepherd the first day, but he did not come. He waited the second day, but still the shepherd did not come. On the third day Djamukh felt a chill of fear.

"Some terrible misfortune must have befallen him if he is not back by now," he said to his friends.

His sharp-eared companion placed his ear to the ground, listened, and said, "The shepherd is in a deep sleep. I can hear the earth tremble as he snores. As for the runner, I'm afraid he will be back any moment."

Sadly Djamukh said, "What shall we do now? It looks as if my head is lost."

Suddenly the black bird with the golden crest swooped down from the sky and perched on Djamukh's shoulder.

"Don't grieve, son of a deer. Many years ago an evil fairy locked me in the stone, saying I should remain there until such time as a brave youth named Djamukh appeared. It is my turn to save you now!"

Leaving an impatient Djamukh behind, the bird flew off. He reached the sleeping shepherd, flew down, and shouted,

"Wake up! Wake up! The life of Djamukh is hanging in the balance, and you sleep!"

The shepherd turned over on the other side and snored even louder. Then the bird began to tickle his nose with his feathers. The shepherd sneezed and awoke. Looking about, he saw the bird, who shook his head and said reproachfully,

"A fine time to sleep! The life of Djamukh is threatened and you lie there like a stone."

The shepherd jumped to his feet. He took the flowers from his bag and started to run. Near the fence of the castle he overtook the giant's runner. In three leaps he reached the entrance where the beautiful girl stood waiting, and placed the flowers in her hands.

Then the youngest warrior, turning to Djamukh, said,

"At the gates of the castle there grows a tall plane tree. Place this plate of water on your head and climb

to the top. If you can do this without spilling any, you may take my sister as your wife."

Djamukh took the plate of water, placed it on his head, and climbed the tree. He climbed out of sight to the very top, and not a drop of water spilled from the plate.

Looking about, he saw wolves far off in the distant mountains attacking the deer that had saved him so many years before. He could not bear to watch and two heavy tears fell from his eyes as he turned his head away. They landed on the hand of the giant warrior standing below.

"Well, this time you have lost!" he exclaimed.

"Why?" asked Djamukh, climbing down. "I did not spill the water."

The warrior extended his hand, and the two drops glistened in the sunlight.

"That is not water, but tears from my heart," answered Djamukh.

The giant touched his lips to the liquid and tasted the salt.

"You are right, Djamukh," he agreed. Turning to his brothers, he said, "This youth deserves to be the husband of our sister. He is not only clever and brave, but has a tender heart as well."

And a great feast was held to celebrate the wedding of the brave and handsome Djamukh to the beautiful girl he had come so far to find.

Hecho
the Lazy

A LONG TIME AGO, in a village in Georgia, lived a very
lazy man. He was so lazy he would do no work at all,
and so he had very little to eat. Finally, unable to stand
his hunger, he decided to seek out the old Gerbat who
keeps the Book of Fate, to ask for help.

After walking many days he reached the home of the
wise man. He took his hat from his head and stood on
the threshold. The Gerbat looked up and saw him and
said,

"Well, Hecho, are you still alive? I should have

thought your laziness would have taken you to your grave by now."

"I am alive, but not satisfied," answered Hecho.

"And why have you come to complain to me?"

"I wish you to change my fate. Tell me how, without working, I can have enough to eat every day."

"So that's what you want! You know it is written, 'what you put into the tureen, your spoon will bring out.' In the Book of Fate it is written that you are doomed to starve if you will not work."

"Are you sure that is what it says?"

"Thus is it written," said the old sage, showing Hecho the huge volume in front of him.

"And who is it wrote that I must starve?" asked Hecho.

"Who wrote it? I wrote it!" answered the Gerbat, glowering.

"Well, if you yourself wrote it, sir, then you are free to cross it out."

For a moment the angry old man was silent. Then he said, "Very well, so be it. I shall help you, lazy one, even though you aren't worth it.

"Return home and wait for the next festival. On the eve of the holiday there will be a storm. When the lightning flashes for the first time, think of something you desire and your wish will be granted. The lightning will flash a second time, and again what you wish for will be granted you. When the lightning flashes for a third time, your last wish will instantly come true. But I know you will not wish for anything worthwhile."

"Why do you say that, good sir?" whined Hecho. "I have already thought of what to ask for. First, I will wish for enough to eat always. Second, I will wish for enough wine, and third, that I find a beautiful and intelligent wife."

"Very well," said the wise old Gerbat. "We shall see if my gifts will be of use to you."

Hecho bowed before the wise man, thanked him for his generosity, and went home.

The evening of the festival he sat on his doorstep and watched the sky. His eyelids started to droop, but Hecho the lazy continued to sit, rubbing his eyes, waiting for the storm.

The dark clouds began to gather and creep toward the high mountains in the quiet valley. Far away the thunder crashed, and the first drops of rain fell on the earth.

Suddenly Hecho's stomach began to ache. Oh, how it hurt! It hurt so much, all Hecho's wishes flew from his head.

"It is certainly the wrong time for this to happen," thought Hecho. "If only this stomach of mine would go away."

Crash! He heard the thunder, and the lightning flashed. Hecho looked down—he had no stomach! At his words it had vanished.

Hecho placed his hands where his stomach had been —nothing was there! Only a spine covered with skin!

Hecho then screeched in a voice hardly his own, "Ai! Ai! What is this? How shall I now eat? It would be better to have too big a stomach than none at all!"

Crash! For a second time he heard thunder. The lightning flashed across the sky, and on Hecho there grew a tremendous stomach. But what a stomach! It was gigantic! It was so big that Hecho fell to the ground, unable to stand on his feet.

Then Hecho shouted at the top of his lungs, "Oh! Oh! Oh! I cannot live with such a stomach. I would be better off as I was before the storm."

Crash! For the third time he heard the thunder and saw the bright flash across the sky. And Hecho was as he had been.

Then the lazy one became angry. Cursing his fate, he ran once more to the Gerbat.

As Hecho rushed along he met a wolf. Old and bedraggled, his sides were so sunken you could almost see through him, and the bones of his spine stuck up like the teeth of a saw.

"Where are you rushing so, dear Hecho?" asked the wolf.

"I am on my way to the wise old Gerbat to tell him about my misfortune."

"Be a good friend, Hecho. Ask him if he can help me, too. No matter how much I eat, I am never satisfied, and I grow thinner and thinner each day."

Hecho agreed, and ran on.

He ran and ran until he could run no more. Near the path he saw an apple tree full of beautiful fruit.

Hecho sat down beneath the tree, picked the largest apple he could find, and greedily bit into it. "Ugh! How sour!" Hecho spat. And he threw the apple on the ground.

The tree wept bitterly and said, "See how I suffer. Everyone who tries my apples says the same thing. And I would be so glad to satisfy the weary travelers who sit beneath me. Couldn't you do something to help me?"

"How would I know how to help you? But I am on my way to the wise Gerbat. I shall ask his advice," said Hecho. And he ran on.

Not far from the house of the Gerbat Hecho became thirsty. He looked about and saw the shining blue ribbon of a stream between the trees. Hecho ran over and knelt beside the clear water. A large fish with an open mouth lay on the sandy bottom.

The fish looked up at Hecho and said, "Good sir, could you not do something to help me? For twenty years I have not been able to close my mouth."

"No," answered Hecho. "But perhaps the wise Gerbat will have some advice for you." And he ran on.

Hecho finally reached the house of the wise man. Looking up from the Book of Fate, the old sage asked, "Have you come to demand still more of me?"

"How can you joke with me this way, sir? You promise to fulfill my dearest wishes and at that very moment you send me an illness."

"You mean you still want to go against fate and be prosperous without working? Very well, I shall make you a gift of great riches. It will be enough for the rest of your life. Go home and you will find it."

"Thank you, kind sir," said Hecho, bowing to the ground.

"Perhaps you have something else to ask of me before you go?" said the Gerbat, smiling wisely.

"That's right," remembered Hecho. "On my way to see you I came upon a fish lying in a stream. For twenty years he has been unable to close his mouth. I promised to ask your advice. How can he rid himself of this terrible misfortune?"

"Under the fish's tongue there lies a precious jewel. When it is taken out, the fish will again be able to close his mouth. Is there anything else?"

"On my way here I passed an apple tree. Its fruit was beautiful but very sour. This tree begged me to ask how to get rid of this terrible misfortune."

"Beneath the roots of this tree a chest is buried. When it is taken out, the apples will taste sweet again. Anything else?"

"I also met a wolf on the way. No matter how much he eats, he grows thinner and thinner each day. I promised to ask how he can rid himself of this misfortune."

"Tell the wolf that in order to fill himself he must eat the most foolish and lazy thing in the world." And the Gerbat slammed the Book of Fate shut.

Happily, Hecho ran home.

As he passed the quiet brook, the fish called to him. "Did you remember to ask the Gerbat about me?"

"He said that under your tongue lies a precious stone. When it is removed, you will be able to close your mouth," replied Hecho.

"Rid me of this misfortune, and as a reward keep the jewel for yourself."

"I have no time to bother with you. The Gerbat said a great fortune is waiting for me," said Hecho. And he ran on.

He came to the apple tree, and the tree called, "What did the Gerbat say?"

"He said that when a chest of gold near your roots is dug up your apples will be sweet again," answered Hecho.

"Then rid me of my misfortune, and as a reward take the gold for yourself," begged the tree.

"I do not want to get my hands dirty. The Gerbat has promised me great riches," said Hecho. And he ran on.

Running as fast as he could, Hecho suddenly saw the wolf lying in the center of the road, barely able to move.

"Did you speak to the Gerbat about me?" he whispered.

Hecho told the wolf about the fish and the apple tree and all that the wise man had said.

"And the Gerbat said I must eat the most foolish and lazy creature in the world?" asked the wolf.

"That's right," answered Hecho.

"In that case," said the wolf, throwing himself upon Hecho, "your final hour has come!"

And he ate him.

How the Donkey
Saved a Village

IN A FARAWAY CITY in Azerbaijan lived a very rich man.
He had an only son named Azhat, who grieved him by
his extravagance. No matter how the father tried to re-
strain his son, it did no good. Finally the old man, unable to bear this, became ill and died of grief.

Azhat quickly went through his rich inheritance. Left
without a penny, he decided to live by his wits. He
caught a magpie and set out for a country where such
birds had never been seen.

Reaching the first village of this country, Azhat

peeped through the window of a house and saw a woman preparing pilaf, a delicious dish of lamb and rice.

When it became dark Azhat went to the door of this house and asked to spend the night. The master of the house was a hospitable fellow, and happily welcomed the unexpected guest, telling his wife to bring them some food.

The woman brought some bread and a little cheese and placed them on the table.

Seeing the plain food, Azhat surreptitiously pinched the magpie hidden under his shirt. The magpie squealed with pain.

"Quiet! This is not the time to give away secrets!" Azhat said severely.

The master of the house asked with amazement, "What kind of bird is that?"

"This is no ordinary bird," replied Azhat. "She knows all the secrets of people. She wished to tell the secrets of your house but I made her keep quiet."

"I beg of you, let the bird speak."

Azhat hit the bird terribly hard and she screeched again.

"The bird says that you are not a good host. In your pantry you have wine and pilaf, yet you serve your guest dry bread and sour cheese."

The man went into the pantry and brought out the pilaf which his wife had hidden at the arrival of their guest.

The mistress of the house reddened with shame, and

said, "Forgive me, I was so busy, I completely forgot about these things. Please help yourself."

After the meal the man begged Azhat to sell him the marvelous bird. Azhat pretended he did not wish to part with the magpie and asked a very high price for her. But the man paid the money willingly, and the following day Azhat left the village.

On the way he bought a donkey, and he rode upon him until he came to a country where such an animal had never been seen. The people of the first village he reached surrounded him on all sides.

"What kind of animal is this? What can it do? How much does it cost?" they clamored.

"This is indeed a marvelous animal," said Azhat. "He protects people from their enemies. But he costs so much, not one of you could afford to buy him."

The inhabitants, who were often preyed upon by a bold band of robbers, decided to buy the valuable animal together, and paid Azhat his price.

Handing over the donkey, Azhat said, "Keep this animal in a dark stable. Feed him only raisins and cold water and never let him out. When the bandits again raid your village, open the door of the stable. In a single moment he will boldly defeat your enemies."

Counting his money, Azhat quickly left the country. Meanwhile the people of the village carried out Azhat's instructions to the letter.

About a month later the band of robbers appeared from the forest. They galloped swiftly into the village.

The inhabitants opened the stable door and sent the

donkey out to meet them. The starving donkey, not having seen the light of day for a long time, galloped out to meet the horses with a wild cry, thinking to find among them the oats he longed for. The robbers, terrified by the wild bray of this strange, fierce-sounding animal, turned swiftly and rode off, never to be seen again.

As for Azhat, he wandered through many lands, living by his wits, until he had amassed a vast fortune. Then he turned his eyes homeward and settled down to live a good and honest life.

The Wise
Liar

THERE WAS ONCE a young Armenian prince named Aran
who was as clever as he was handsome. His father, de-
feated by strong enemies, had died, leaving him only
a silver dagger. Aran decided to sell the dagger and
seek his fortune in distant lands.

On his way to the bazaar he met a merchant who
admired the dagger and said, "I have here a purse
filled with gold. It will be yours if you can tell the most
incredible story and make me acknowledge it is not
true. But if you cannot make me say that you lie, the
dagger will be mine."

76

Aran agreed, and began his tale.

"Once I had nine hundred swarms of bees. Among my bees was one that was blind and another that was lame. Every morning, before allowing them out of their hives, and at the end of the day upon their return, I counted my bees.

"One evening I found the lame bee missing. What was I to do? I seated myself on the blind bee and went in search of the lame one. I rode far and finally found the missing bee. A farmer had caught him, harnessed him to a plow, and was turning the soil in his garden.

"I became angry with the farmer and asked him to pay me for the work of my bee. We quarreled for a long time, until finally he agreed to give me half of all that grew in his garden.

"He had six watermelons there. I took my share, and loading the three melons on the lame bee, I then mounted the blind one and started for home.

"I rode to the gate, but the melons were too big to take through it. What was I to do? I decided to cut the melons in half. As soon as I had split the first one, a nut tree started to grow from its center. I climbed the tree, and at the very top I found a jug full of butter. I reached in to take the butter out and felt a chain inside. I pulled at the chain and drew out forty camels loaded with gold.

"I recognized them immediately as the camels stolen from my father when I was still a child. Overjoyed at my good fortune, I took the camels and started for

home. On the way, however, I was attacked by a fierce band of robbers who stole all my wealth, including that very purse you hold in your hand."

"You're lying!" screamed the merchant.

"Well, if you say I am lying, the purse is mine," answered Aran calmly.

The merchant reddened in anger and flung the purse at Aran. The young prince tucked the purse in his coat and continued on his way. A king, however, had overheard his story while riding by, and shouted after him. "Stop, stop, young man!"

Aran turned and the king said, "Give me the purse."

Aran did not wish to give it up but there was nothing else for him to do. The monarch was surrounded by his many guards and if he were not to obey, they would surely take it by force.

"You are a very quick-witted fellow," said the king. "I shall give you thirty days to think of a most incredible story and make me acknowledge it as a lie. If you can do this, I shall return this purse to you, and in addition, make you a gift of this golden ball. But if you are unable to make me say you lie, your head will fall from your shoulders!"

Aran was angry, and he thought, "Very well, great king! We shall see who wins!" He went to a potter and asked him to make a pitcher that would hold forty pounds of gold.

At the end of the thirty days the pitcher was ready and Aran placed it on his shoulder and set off for the palace.

Seeing Aran with his tremendous pitcher, the king asked, "Why have you brought such a large vessel with you, young man?"

"You owe my father forty pounds of gold and I have come to collect it," said Aran.

"You lie!" shouted the king furiously.

"Well, if you say I am lying, return my purse and give me the golden ball," calmly answered Aran.

The king did not wish to part with his favorite plaything, but there was nothing else he could do. It was better to give Aran the purse and ball than forty pounds of gold.

The clever prince pocketed his treasures and continued on his way to seek his fortune.

The Young Storyteller

THE YOUNG MAN SIGHED as the storyteller finished. "There seems no end to your stories," he said. "They fall as easily from your lips as the blood from the wolf I killed this morning.

"I'd like to ride into the mountains with you, old man," he continued, "to be welcomed by the children as we approach the village, to be greeted by their fathers with hospitality and warmth. But when the nights are cold and we sit before the fire, how do I begin?"

"It really isn't hard to tell a story," said the old man. "Start with a hero—a fierce khan, or a simple shepherd, or even an animal."

"How about a rooster?" asked the young man. "Can a rooster be a hero—a puffed-up, strutting, proud and pompous rooster? When I was a child I heard a Tatar tale about a bird like that."

"Tell it now," said the old storyteller.

And the young man began.

The Radiant
Khan

IN A BARNYARD lived a rooster.

He strutted about, surveying his domain, seeing that all was in order and putting on airs.

Early in the morning he jumped up onto the high fence, and shouted:

"Cock-a-doodle-doo! Cock-a-doodle-doo! I am the shah rooster, khan rooster, sultan rooster! Dear hens, black, white, and golden! Who on this earth is the most beautiful of all?"

The hens all came running, stepped up to their glori-

ous shah, radiant khan, mightiest sultan in all the world, and sang:

"Where, where, where, glorious shah? Where, where, where, radiant khan? Where, where, where, mightiest sultan, can anyone be found to equal you? There is no one in the world braver than you, no one in the world wiser than you, no one in all the world more beautiful than you!"

"Cock-a-doodle-doo! Cock-a-doodle-doo!" still louder crowed the rooster. "Who has a voice louder than a lion? Whose legs are stronger than iron? Who has a more brightly colored coat?"

"You, our shah, have the brightest coat. You, our khan, have legs strong as iron. You, our sultan, have a voice louder than a lion!" sang the hens.

The rooster, swollen with pride, lifted his comb and crowed with all his might:

"Cock-a-doodle-doo! Cock-a-doodle-doo! You women, come closer and tell me. Whose throne is the highest? On whose head sits the tallest crown?"

The hens came nearer to the fence and bowing low to the pompous rooster sang:

"Your throne is the highest of all. On your head, your crown glows like fire. You, our only shah! You, our radiant khan! You, our mighty sultan!"

While the preening rooster stood proudly surveying his adoring audience, a fat cook crept up quietly behind the fence and grabbed him by the leg.

She killed the great shah with a sharp knife. She plucked the dazzling coat from the radiant khan. And from the mightiest sultan in all the world she made a delicious soup.

And the admiring dinner guests all exclaimed:

"Never was there such a marvelous rooster! Never was there such a tasty rooster."

The old man laughed. "He wasn't much of a hero, that one. But I like your story. Rooster or man, I've known many like that."

And the two storytellers mounted their horses and rode up the steep path.